The O G Pimp from West Palm Beach, Part I

Kevin 'Big Papa' Guyton

The O G Pimp From West Palm Beach, Part I
Copyright ©2010 by Kevin 'Big Papa' Guyton
ISBN 9-781-4563274-8-4

Cover art by Joshua Dunbar
Joshuadunbar.com

This novel is based on true events, however some names, geography and time frames have been changed which makes this a work of fiction. Any resemblance to real people, deceased or alive, actual events, entities, establishments, and/or locations are only intended to provide the story with a sense of reality and authenticity. Names, characters, places and events are either a product of the author's imagination or are used fictitiously as are those fictionalized occurrences that may involve real people and did not happen or are simply set in the future.

THE WOLF'S CALL

Wolves have an extraordinary strength,
In a cell, tame it will not become,
Laying dormant the blood thirst of a hustler,
A full moon hears his soul as it cries,

Under his vision you clearly lie,
In his sense of smell you try to hide,
He heard your high heels caress the street,
Savoring the cheap perfume of a future encounter
when we meet,

His prey heard the wolf's call BIG PAPA!
And the alphabet boys gave an AAA+ critique,
In a town of sunsets on beaches,
A trick's thirst for sex made her unique!

A whore's capabilities are untold,
The guard on his heart he had to put,
Sometimes he would have to look twice,
He would see the wolf come out as being nice!

Foreword

At the age of sixteen years old, I started hustling in Palm Beach, Florida. My mom had six boys and one girl. She was very strict on going to church. Mom raised us up as Baptists. We lived on the South end of Riviera Beach, in a two bedroom house which is located in Palm Beach.

In 1968 we moved to a middle-class neighborhood in Monroe Heights. It had four bedrooms, two bathrooms and a pool. Moms provided very well for us with the help of dad. I chose the street life out of curiosity.

In the ninth grade I managed to get suspended from all public schools in the county. My success for night school wasn't great either. I started hanging with my brother, "G.W." He tried to install the school in me.

I took on his ways only because the girls flocked to him. G.W. was manipulative with all the women. I admired that about G.W. God bless the dead. When I saw how my brother could make women do anything he wanted and give him their money as well, my life started going in a whole new direction...

Here's my story.

Chapter 1

1974

At the young age of sixteen, I was hanging down at the bar on Dixie Highway in Riviera Beach. I went outside to see a taxi pull up and a young woman step out. I went up to the sexy black woman and introduced myself.

"What's your name?" I asked her.

"Monty!" She said in an impressive voice.

"Would you like a drink?"

"Yeah, sure," She said before we went inside and sat at the bar together.

Once inside, I asked her where she was from.

"Jupiter." She responded, as in Jupiter, Florida. "I live with my brother across on South Ave."

We talked and took more shots. I asked her, "Do you have a job?"

"Yeah, at the Holiday in on Singer Island. How 'bout you?"

"I work as a dishwasher over at Berdine's."

A few hours went by and Monty asked me, "Will you walk me home?"

"Yeah," I told her. And we left.

The following weekend we met up at the bar called Two Spot.

"Baby girl, let's get drinks."

See, back then Two Spot was a bar that all under age teenagers could go and buy alcohol, smoke and buy weed. Monty started telling me about how guys at her job always complimented her on her looks; specifically, her body.

Monty was a bad bitch. She was dark-skinned, 5'9", one hundred and forty pounds with a nice big ass and just the right size juicy tittles. Monty's hair was low-cut, faded on the sides. And she still was a bad bitch.

That night we got a room in West Palm Beach at a spot called Queens Lodge. After checking into our room we saw a blonde headed white girl posted as a prostitute. I stood out on the balcony looking down at the blonde head. She looked up and nodded. Monty came out on the balcony to make a jealous statement out of the blue.

"I can make more money than that bitch any day or time."

We went back to chill on the bed. Monty just undid my pants and took me into her mouth, deep-throating me. Looking up at me like she would eat me alive. Pushing me back on the bed sucking my balls, she then started licking my ass. I didn't know that she was a freak like that. I took as much as I

The O G Pimp From West Palm Beach, Part I

could, then jumped up. Monty was a freaky ass bitch, ya heard me. Monty turned me out just that fast. I laid her down and fucked the shit out of her. Monty bent over doggy-style so I could dig deep off into her pussy. Then she took the dick out of herself and put it right into her asshole. From that moment on I was Butt man.

After we finished we took a shower and chilled. Still drinking and smoking Monty looked at me and said, "I want to tell you something."

I said, "Go ahead."

"First you have to promise you won't leave or get mad."

"Bet." I agreed.

"The money I used to pay for the room didn't come from my checkbook."

"Well where did it come from?"

"I give my checks to my brother to pay the rent. The money came from this white guy on Singer Island at the Holiday Inn where I work."

"How much did you get from him?"

She grabbed her bag and pulled out what was left. "Four hundred dollars," She answered, then gave it to me.

"So you fucked him for this?"

"Yes, I did." Monty said.

I left it at that and said, "I still love you. But only as what you are. And that's a hoe." I wanted her to be my woman but she was a whore. So it was what it was. My mind started clicking.

"If we do this, we do it right." I told her.

"Okay," She said.

"Bring me all your money and I will protect you at all times."

We walked to the store and there were cars blowing their horns to get her attention. She was that bad of a bitch.

"Handle your business and meet me back at the room."

Thirty or forty minutes later, she met back up with me and put three hundred dollars in my hand. I saw the blonde white bitch standing in her doorway. So it became clear to me that I didn't turn Monty out. She turned me out. Monty started a whole new life for me. I didn't chose pimping, it chose me.

Monty went and talked the blonde into working with her for me. And the blonde agreed.

We sat down and Blondie told me, "I'm from Orlando and need somebody to look after me."

"If my man looks after you, bring him all your money."

Monty was cold-blooded with her shit. Blondie pulled her pants off and pulled out a plastic bag from her pussy. She gave me three hundred and fifty dollars and said, "I have no problem with that.

The O G Pimp From West Palm Beach, Part I

I don't deal with black guys because they take their money back. Oh, my name is Crystal."

"I'm Kevin, your pimp."

Crystal had a car which was hers; A Toyota. She was 5'10" and one hundred and twenty-five pounds. She had nice titties, ocean-blue eyes and was well spoken.

Monty and Crystal hit the streets as a team and this is where my life began as a real pimp. I kept my .25 pistol to look after my hoes. A few months went by as Monty and Crystal continued humpin' to make my money. Life was good.

Monty, Crystal and I moved into an apartment two streets over from mom's crib in Monroe Heights. Crystal and Monty had built up so much clientele, that they would have no problem meeting in special places or at certain times.

One day Monty came and asked me, "Can I use your twenty-five automatic. I need it for this date with these two black guys."

"Baby girl, if you need a gun for a date them maybe you shouldn't go."

"I know one of them; I just want to protect myself." I gave her the gun and she left.

Crystal and I started talking more. Then she took off her clothes for me to fuck her. I obliged.

Chapter 2

A few hours went by and Monty returned with five hundred dollars and a safe. One thing that I always drilled in my hoes' head was to always remember where you go with a 'John', just in case I have to enforce a situation that may get out of hand.

Monty had gotten comfortable with the two black guys "tricking" on her so she told me, "They would like for Crystal to come next time."

"When?" I asked Monty.

"Tonight and I don't need the gun. They seem alright."

Crystal was up for it so we went over everything. Mostly, 'remember where you go'. I rolled up some weed to smoke and Monty asked me, "What do you want me to do if I find another girl?"

"That's not important — Do what you do. Trick, that's it."

The girls went out to meet up with their dates. They were picked up in a small green car. I thought it looked familiar but dismissed the thought and smoked the rest of my weed.

Three hours later, my hoes walked back to our spot. They came in the door exhausted, upset, shocked and humiliated. Right then I knew that something had went wrong. Monty explained the game that had been ran on them. Crystal said, "They paid us all our money, but in the end they took it all back."

I was so mad that I beat the shit out of them. Then said to myself, 'this is a test.' I got my gun and put my clothes on. Then Monty told me where they were. At the time I was trained by Mark Herman of the DoJo on Kamattis in West Palm Beach. Monty grabbed her knife and Crystal did the same.

Keep in mind, I'm seventeen years old, big and over two hundred pounds. About to handle the situation at hand. How some muther fuckas gon' disrespect me and my hoes. Not seeing this as my first real test as a pimp, but it was. I jumped in the car and told them, "Chill, y'all just chill."

I drove over to Rosemary's. It took me ten minutes. It was dark, hustlers were everywhere getting money. Hoes were on the stroll. All types of activity was jumping on Rosemary. It was the strip, always jumping.

When I got to the house I parked the car across the street on Ford and Rosemary.

The O G Pimp From West Palm Beach, Part I

One of the guys was sitting out front. I had my .25 auto in my pocket and my bat in my hand. When I walked into the gate he didn't notice who I was. I asked him, "Did a white and black chic' come by a few hours ago?"

As soon as he said, "Yeah!" I hit him with the bat in his head.

He hit the ground real hard. I thought I killed him but I didn't. I let him get up. Then pulled my gun out. Someone hit me from behind with a two-by-four. It was the other black guy. Some guy came outside yelling, "Aren't you G.W.'s brother?"

I said, "Yeah."

He told them, "This fight is going to be one-on-one."

After the two guys heard who I was, they apologized and paid me all my money. I got in my car and left to meet back up with my hoes. They were so happy I made it back.

"I got all the money, and it won't happen again," I told them. Due to the fact that the guy who I hit with the bat had to go get stitches.

From that point on I let them know there would be no more dealing with black Johns unless I confirmed it.

Chapter 3

Back at the apartment, Monty started talking about her life.

"One day this guy named Derrick came by our house looking for my brother Tony. So I let him in. I told Derrick that Tony wasn't home. So he noticed that I was by myself. I was only twelve years old at the time. He pushed me down on the couch and took my virginity. He told me to be quiet and don't scream. So I did what he said. He pumped into me until I started to bleed. I was so scared I just layed there without crying, yelling or saying stop. After he got done, my legs had blood all on them and he told me, 'You bet not tell nobody'. Then he gave me a dollar and left.

"I got up to clean myself off then cried and laid in the bed. Then I started chilling at this chill spot in Jupiter where Derrick used to come get me, have sex with me then give me a dollar and drop me off. The place was called the Tree. I would sit there at the Tree and smoke weed, drink and try to play pool. About six months later, I was at home chilling and my brother Tony started looking at me noticing how my body had started developing more. Then Tony said, 'I heard that you and Derrick was fuckin.' I didn't say anything. I just sat there. Tony looked at me and said 'If you don't let me do it to you I'm going to tell momma. I just gave in and let Tony do as he pleased. He took both our clothes off, then got on top of me and started pushing his dick in and out of me. I started to feel pain so I started crying and telling Tony that he was hurting me. Tony didn't pay me no mind and didn't stop.

"A few weeks went by and he was still doing it to me. After Tony found out Derrick was only giving me one dollar he told me that I don't have to sell my body for one dollar and gave me a twenty. And told me that he would buy me new clothes and shoes. He told me to stop having sex with Derrick or he would tell momma. So I stopped sleeping with him and stopped seeing him at all."

Monty went on to explain that years later this guy named Doodabug had opened up an after-hour spot for the young crowd; and named it after himself. All of the young people, including herself would go there to chill. She started getting the attention of Doodabug eventually because remember, Monty is a bad ass bitch. Doodabug would let her in for free and give her drinks plus weed. After a while he talked her into chilling with him one night. One thing led to another and Monty was getting some of the best head in her life by Doodabug.

Chapter 4

Monty had her first orgasm and fell head over heels for Doodabug. Then he would get on top of Monty and fuck the shit out of her for a while until she came again or he came first. Monty would let him teach her how to deep-throat his dick until he came down her throat.

After that session, for some reason, Monty says she stayed in touch with Doodabug all the time.

"One Friday night I was chilling at the bar with Doodabug and he told me he had two other guys with him who wanted some pussy from my fine ass. I'd never been with three before but I said 'fuck it'. Okay.

"Doodabug and his friends went to get a room for us to do this. As we got into the room clothes started coming off. One of the white guys put his dick in my mouth and down my throat, making me choke and gag. Then Doodabug laid me on the bed and pinned my legs all the way back. Then lowered his dick into my asshole. I started to shift and try to come from up under him but he held me tighter and went harder. I tried to take what I could but by the time I was about to say something, he came in my ass.

"The next white guy told me he wanted to me to ride him so I did. I climbed on top to ride his dick and felt how big it was. I tried to go down slow but he pulled me down as hard as he could, up and down until he came.

After they got done, I was feeling some kind of way because I was confused about pain or feeling good. My asshole was hurting and bleeding. My mind just to told me to go with the flow and I did for the rest of the night.

"I got out of the bed and showered after we finished. I still felt pain, but it felt good too. This experience was unforgettable. They gave me three hundred dollars and took me home." Monty finished.

She went on to tell the couple of listeners that back at home, her brother Tony started having her suck his dick all the time. For that to be his real sister he was a sick young man; but hey, shit happens Kevin thought to himself.

Two years later Monty's mom helped her get a job with this white lady cleaning houses. Here a lot of white men noticed how bad her body was. They started paying her to fuck and suck them off. They would give her large sums of money. Monty loved to see her men's faces when they got ready to come.

Chapter 5

Meanwhile, Monty ended up meeting this young guy from the neighborhood named Will. The both of them started seeing each other for a while and it was good.

Monty never told Will she was a trick. When she finally decided to tell him about it, it was too late because she was pregnant. Monty kept it to herself. Will always took care of Monty when she was pregnant. She eventually stopped tricking before she had the baby. Her brother would also help out a lot with the money and clothes but still made her give him some head; although he stopped fucking her.

Will stayed with a job and helped her out a lot with everything. But he was over-protective to the point where it started to get out of hand. So once Monty had the baby she bought her own house and paid all the bills. A few months after the baby was born, Monty told Will, "It's not going to work out because you're too jealous and over-protective. So, it's over."

"Okay," Will agreed. "I can't make you stay."

Will started seeing another woman after the breakup so Monty explained that she had to find another place. Because since he paid all the bills she felt that it was his house. She left feeling fucked up thinking, 'He didn't even give me no money. Fuck it; I'll take care of my daughter by myself.'

Monty went back to Doodabug for some support and did a few tricks on the side to take care of her daughter. Monty named the lil' girl Sara. Her brother Tony moved back to Palm Beach so she and Sara could have a place to stay. This is where she met Kevin.

Back at the apartment Crystal said, "That was a touching story," then rolled up some weed and opened up some Colt 45's and MD 20/20's.

The horn blew outside for Crystal. This white guy was in a Mercedes with three other guys. Tee came in the house, pulled out a bank roll of money and said, "I'll give them whatever they want."

Kevin asked Tee, "Where y'all going?"

"To the Holiday Inn," Tee replied.

"That's where I used to work," Monty chimed in.

"Who are they in the car?" Crystal asked.

"Those are my real estate partners. Plus they have a lot of money like me and want to have fun."

Monty and Crystal left with them and Kevin counted the money. It was about fifteen hundred

The O G Pimp From West Palm Beach, Part I

dollars. By the time they got to the room Tee told Monty, "If your man wants to be closer to y'all, we have another room next door."

"I'll call him," Crystal responded. And she dialed Kevin back at home.

Kevin came right away and chilled next door. He was prepared for a weekend affair, because that's how long Crystal told him they had the room for over the phone.

Once she got off the phone with Kevin, Crystal started snorting powder while Monty smoked her weed before the session started.

One guy started fucking Monty doggy-style while the other two guys had Crystal on all fours with one cock in her ass pounding away and one in her mouth making her gag.

The whole weekend was a non-stop fucking session. Tee and his boys fucked the shit out of Crystal and Monty. Crystal got knocked down so hard that she had to go to the hospital because her pussy and anus was scary swollen. She'd taken too much dick for a day and now had to pay the price of a trip to the doctor. Monty was worn out as well but her body was good. Before leaving for the hospital, Tee's crew gave the girls one thousand dollars. Then Kevin took them to be taken care of. Crystal ended up staying in St. Mary's for about four to five days. Not that she required that much attention, but the nurses saw to it that this poor white child got rested before heading back to the streets.

Chapter 6

After Crystal came home from St. Mary's she was paid a visit by one of Tee's friends.

"We got a little carried away off the powder. We just had to get this message to you." The speaker gave her two thousand dollars and left.

Later that year, Crystal started dating Tee's friend on the regular. At least once per week. Troy had a lot of money. And a few times he'd tried to get Crystal to run off with him. Come to find out, he was married with two kids back in Daytona Beach where they lived.

"Come with me. I'll get you a new car, house, and enough money to take care of you." He used to beg.

And every time she'd tell him, "I have to ask Kevin first."

One night she asked Kevin. And he told her, "He can buy you whatever he wants, but you're not leaving."

Troy ended up buying her a brand new Cadillac. But Crystal gave it to Kevin as a gift. She eventually asked him, "Can I go visit Troy in Daytona?"

"Yeah," he answered.

When Crystal arrived in Daytona's airport, Troy was there to pick her up and drove her to the Howard Johnson's.

Troy tried to keep Crystal around by making love to her and buying her anything he thought she'd want while in town. She stayed for a few days then headed back home to tell Monty and Kevin how it was.

"He sexed me all weekend. We stayed at the Howard's and he bought me all this shit I got," She told them as she showed them her gifts. "He told me that he would buy me another car and a house plus give me more money. He took me to meet his family as well. I felt so special for a moment. Especially when I look into his eyes. What should I do?" She asked Kevin.

"What do you want to do?" He asked her.

Crystal responded by saying, "I will do whatever you want me to."

"Tell Troy to buy you a car and a condo. And to put some money in your banking account. Tell him you're in a thirty thousand dollar bind with your pimp and if he pays it you can go."

Crystal told Troy Kevin's exact words. Troy told her "No problem."

After about a week or two, everything was done.

The O G Pimp From West Palm Beach, Part I

Troy bought her a new car and put the money in the trunk. He drove to their apartment and gave her the keys to the car. He told her, "The money is in the trunk. I will see you in two weeks. Bye."

Kevin took the money out of the trunk and took it into the crib to count every dollar.

He told Monty, "Go with Crystal to help her settle in."

Two weeks later they were in a new crib just like he had said. He took the both of them shopping and gave them pocket money before showing them around. The next three days brought the end of the fun. Because Monty was about to go back home. And she would tell Kevin of all the fun she had in Daytona, and to give Kevin a report on Troy.

"He tried to spoil us with all this shit. This ain't what I want to talk to you about though. Troy hooked Crystal up with one of his cousins who is on dope real bad."

About thirty days later, Crystal had started using real bad and got turned out. Kevin hadn't heard a word from Crystal and was starting to get worried.

Chapter 7

Kevin told his cousin Big D, his homeboy Kenny and Monty that, "We going to get Crystal. Because some shit ain't right."

Kenny drove and carried his gun because he had a permit to do so. A few hours on the road they pulled up to this big ass house with the black gates around it. The guards tried calling inside to see if the visitors could come inside but got no answer.

"Look, it's a surprise for her birthday," Monty lied to the guard.

With that he let them pass go.

Kevin knocked on the door and Crystal answered, with a shocked surprise on her face.

"What the fuck is going on with you?" Kevin barged in and asked.

Crystal just stood there.

Then Kevin said, "You all drugged up and look like you're about to die.

You don't look like yourself. What the fuck is going on?"

Her body was worn down. Crystal was looking unusually bad. Before she said anything some redhead girl came out and started to speak but Monty cut her off and asked Crystal, "Why you haven't been calling or came back to see us?"

Kevin grabbed her by the arm and pulled her into another room and smacked the shit out of her asking, "What the fuck is going on? Don't lie. Or I'mma do something to make you wish you hadn't of."

Crystal began to cry and explain, "I started using powder real bad. Then the redhead girl, Susan turned me out on dope. One thing led to another, then I started shooting up."

Kevin grabbed her hand and pushed up the sleeve of her house coat to reveal her arm, checking for shoot-up marks. He didn't find any.

"I shoot it up my pussy."

"What! Fuck that, we goin' home before this shit kills you."

Kevin and Crystal walked back to the living room. There Crystal said, "Look, y'all can go back home and let me deal with this, okay."

"What's wrong with you? You don't want to come back with us?" Monty asked offended.

"Just trust me. I'll see y'all soon." Crystal said.

"Okay then. We gon', just make sure you deal with it." Kevin said before walking out.

The O G Pimp From West Palm Beach, Part I

A week had passed and no one still hadn't heard from Crystal. She sent about eight thousand through the mail after about two weeks but still failed to surface. Two days after the money had come Kevin got a call about Crystal saying she'd died from an overdose. She was in the condo. He gave the news to Monty and all hell broke loose.

After allowing his anger to boil over, Kevin set off to find Troy. He was going to kill him to get some revenge for his prized whore. When he got to the condo, Troy was nowhere to be found. But Dirty Red was there. After beating the shit out of Dirty Red, Kevin made her call Troy on the phone.

"I don't understand how she overdosed," Troy plead bull-shitingly. "But I'll give you a large sum of money along with Dirty Red to compensate you for her death."

Kevin took the money, his new hoe Dirty Red, and Monty and moved into another hotel. He knew that Red knew more than what she was telling. So he pressed her.

"What the hell is going on that you're not telling me?"

"I don't know nothing else," Red lied.

Monty jumped up and started whooping on her. He beat the shit out her for a couple of minutes before Dirty Red started talking.

"Troy wanted to have control over us. And he told me to get her strung out on dope as much as I could."

"I'm gon' kill this nigga," Kevin threatened. Then called Big D. and Kenny and told Red and Monty, "We need to leave because it's about to get hot." The crew went back to Palm Beach then Kevin called Troy again and told him, "I know what happened between you and Crystal. I thought you loved her. You owe me big time."

"Okay." Troy responded. "Whatever you want. Just don't hurt me."

"Alright." Kevin told Troy. Then started working Red overtime.

Big D. and Kenny had drove back home. Back at Queens Lodge Monty and Red decided to get money all day, non-stop before Kevin came back for the day. Dirty Red had been acting kind of sick so she came back and told Kevin, "I need some boy. I'm dope sick."

"You're a stone cold junkie now with a habit. I'll get you some dope every twelve hours." He proceeded to go downtown to Rosemary's to see his connect and get her some dope to speedball.

Six months later, Dirty Red had started making enough money to where Monty could just chill and fuck Kevin a lot more. Dirty Red had went on a date with these two rich, white guys. They got so

The O G Pimp From West Palm Beach, Part I

busy having their way with her that they didn't notice her stealing their shit. Three hours later, Red came back with five hundred dollars and two Rolex watches. Kevin took the money and both watches and asked, "Where did these watches come from?"

"I just took them," Red said. "I want you to have them."

"No, take 'em back." He told her. But she didn't make a move to grab them, and she didn't force them on him. "I'll go check them out to see if they're the real deal, first." Kevin said.

He went to the nearest jewelry dealer to have them checked out. And that's just what they did. The watches checked out to be real. So he kept them for himself.

Kevin and the girls stayed in the room for another three weeks before the police came knocking. Evidently, the two tricks that Red took the watches from had taken pictures of her. And sent the police looking for her. She wasn't hard to find because she'd checked in with her true identification at the front desk. So the clerk sent them to their room. Red was the prime suspect in a Robbery case.

"Take these watches back!" Kevin told her when she walked in from working. "Those Johns sent the police."

"Baby don't give them back, No matter what. Even if I go to jail, I want you to have them as my gift."

The next day, the police caught Red on her stroll and locked her up. About six hours after getting locked up, Kevin was there to bond her out. He did so and they all left. And went back to his Riviera Beach apartment. After settling in, Kevin went down to the Old Dixie Riviera Beach Life liquor store. Where he bumped into a detective.

"I'm looking for one of your girls. Kim, a-k-a Dirty Red. She needs to turn herself in."

Three days later Curly Joe, the detective called Kevin's phone and said, "It's about a robbery case. She missed her court date."

Kevin waited until Red came back and asked her, "Why did you miss your court date?"

"Because I'm going to take the five years they offered me. I want to get clean. I figure that's a good start."

That night, Kevin, Monty and Red had a threesome all night long. The next day Red turned herself in. A few days passed and Kevin took it upon himself to get Monty and go visit Red. He also put two thousand dollars on her books.

Monty had been making more money since Red was gone. She and Kevin spent the next five years fucking, sucking and thinking about old Red. By

The O G Pimp From West Palm Beach, Part I

the time Red got out she was clean. And Kevin and Monty were there to pick her

up. But right then and there she said, "I don't want this life no more. I'm asking if I can just go back to Daytona with my mom and start over."

Kevin looked at Kim and said, "At least you're serious. And yeah, you can go."

Kim left and went back with her mom. Kevin heard no more from Kim, a.k.a. Pretty Red, a.k.a. Dirty Red, a.k.a. Susan.

Chapter 8

Back at Riviera Beach Kevin started looking for a cat named Tom because he owed him some money for a pound of weed that he never paid for. He ended up catching the youngster at Sun Coast High School in the bathroom smoking. Kevin put hands on him right on the spot. He beat Tom to a stand- still and walked out. He was able to move in and out like this because Kevin himself was still around the average age of high schoolers.

Kevin went back to the apartment and told Monty what had just happened. She told him, "Watch that nigga. He will call the police."

I guess he was damned. Because three weeks later the police showed up at his door and arrested him for robbery.

Kevin was sent to the detention center for six months. Then went to the Okeechobee Boys School until he was eighteen. After that he was released. He went back home and got up with Monty again. When he did catch back up with her she was in the midst of fucking like never before. They hooked up and fucked for a while before

Kevin noticed that she wasn't the same Monty he knew before. She even started to "act funny". So they called it quits.

A few weeks after splitting with Monty, Kevin ran into a guy named Jim who started to sell weed for him. Unfortunately, Jim fucked up about five pounds of weed. He paid some of the money then told Kevin, "I ain't paying the rest."

Kevin snapped and beat the shit out of Jim with a pole. And walked off on him laying. Jim ended up telling the cops and sending Kevin on the run for about six months until it blew over.

He went to Dunbar Village to live with his brother, Aldanson. He got Kevin a job as a bouncer at a bar called the Castle. The Castle was located on Tamaran and had apartments built on top of it. Kevin got free room and board plus all he could eat at the restaurant inside the bar. The man who owned it all was named Bernard Laton. He also owned a small store. Kevin paid Bernard an additional fifty dollars for rent on his own.

One night, Kevin was going into his apartment and heard a loud moaning coming from another apartment. He thought to himself, damn somebody is fuckin' the shit out of her. Kevin eased closer to hear more. She moaned louder and louder the closer he got. Then he heard, "Shut up bitch!"

The O G Pimp From West Palm Beach, Part I

The lady responded by saying, "Fuck this shit. I'm not going to keep fucking all of you."

Smack! Was all Kevin heard after that. Then more moans. "Stop, stop. I fucked you, you and sucked their dicks while he fucked me in the ass all hard. I'm done."

Inside, one guy started fucking her in the ass even harder while one guy fucked her face. Then she yelled, "Stop, please stop!"

Kevin grabbed his gun from his waistband and kicked the door in. He saw one guy in her mouth and one in her ass. He saw four guys around her then asked, "Do you want to be here?"

"No, I don't." The girl answered.

"Well, tell them you're my hoe."

"I'm his hoe." She said.

"Get up and get your shit." Kevin told her. "Let's go."

She got up and grabbed her clothes and walked out with Kevin. They went back to his apartment and talked.

"My name is Pam. Thank you for helping me out. I'll always be a very thankful hoe for you."

"That's good. I'm Kevin. Go take a shower and get yourself together."

After Pam got out of the shower, Kevin began to explain how he got down.

And Pam told him, "Look, I had a pimp. But this is how I got caught up in this bullshit. I smoke crack and my pimp did too. He told me to come over here with him so that we could get high. Then he told me that I would be able to chill for a few days as well. Then Tony, my pimp just sold me for some crack to those guys and left me there. And they took me for their fuck slave. Then you came."

"Look, if you can't be real with me and make money for me then you need to leave right now."

"No, it's cool. I got your back and will do whatever you need me to do. I'm your hoe now daddy."

Pam was 5'10" and about one hundred and forty pounds. She had long blonde hair and blue eyes. Kevin took her down to Super Stars, the corner store to show her off. She worked it well. The owner was Sam, but we called him Super Star; after his store. Sam pulled Kevin to the side and asked who she was.

"Pam!" He called her over. "This is Star. I want you to go with him."

Star handed Pam two hundred dollars and she gave it to Kevin.

"Go to the back and wait for her," He told Sam.

Sam went behind the counter. Pam went in after him. He led her to his office. Then put on a condom, bent her over doggy-style and fucked the dog shit out of her until he came.

The O G Pimp From West Palm Beach, Part I

Pam came back out with another hundred dollars and gave it to Kevin. Sam came back to the front and Kevin handed him some items to ring up.

"No, that's on the house," Sam waved him off.

Chapter 9

When they got back to the apartment, Pam went and took a shower. Afterwards, she came out ass naked and gave Kevin an envelope with eighteen thousand dollars inside. Pam told Kevin, "While Star was so busy hitting my shit from the back I was busy seeing what I could get out of him as well." Pam started calling Kevin Daddy from that day on.

Kevin pushed her back on the bed because he was hard as hell. He ate her pussy so good that all you heard was, "Oh daddy, don't stop, oh shit. I'm cuming."

Kevin climbed on top of Pam and pushed her legs all the way back and long-stroked her until she came again. Then he flipped her over and fucked her doggy-style for a few.

"Daddy, let me ride that dick like a cowgirl."

Kevin laid on his back to let Pam climb on top and she rode him like never before. Then she got up and started deep-throating him so good he couldn't take it no more. He came down her throat and she swallowed like a pro. Kevin bent her back over and fucked her so good that he felt her pussy muscles pulling him.

"Bitch who pussy is this?"

"It's your pussy daddy. It's yours" She screamed over and over until she came all over his dick.

He took his dick out of her pussy and slid it into her ass real slow. Then eased in and out to get her in the mood.

"Daddy take this ass right now. Take it," She gave in.

He pounded away hard, deep and fast until he was about to cum. And pulled out of her tight asshole as she turned around and caught it all on her face.

After another shower session they sat on the bed. Kevin opened up a Colt 45 as she lit up some weed.

"My father has a Seafood store on Military Trail." She began to tell him. "Daddy I know how to get into my father's safe."

"Why the fuck would you steal from your father?" He asked her.

"He cast me out of our family after the relationship didn't work with the guy he chose for me to marry. So fuck him. I know how to get in with the codes so I don't have to worry about getting caught. We can take all the money."

"Don't trip. We'll get back to that later. First I want to talk about that car you say you had."

"It's a white Vette, at the house with my ex-husband."

"Whose name is the car in?"

"Mine."

"We need that car. Let's go get it."

Kevin and Pam took a taxi to the West Gate area. They pulled up to the house to see Russell, her ex along with three other men dressed in dirty boots and fisherman attire looking through the cab.

"What the fuck you doing with this nigger in front of my house?" Russell yelled as they stepped out of the taxi.

"First of all, he's not a nigger, he's my man. And I came to get my car."

"You ain't gettin' no car from here. You can get your ass off my lot."

"Look, we ain't leavin' without the car," Kevin said.

"I'm calling the police," Russell spat.

"Shit, that's a good idea."

The police arrived in record time. Then told Russell, "Look, if the car is in her name then it's hers and she is free to leave with it." Kevin and Pam then got into the snow-white Corvette and left.

After about two months they moved to Riviera in a motel called Barbrazon. And like always, Kevin got another room for Pam to trick out of. But unlike his other hoes, Pam made herself a work schedule. She'd work from five to seven p.m., twelve to two a.m. and six a.m. until twelve noon. Money came super fast.

One day while on the strip, an officer stopped Pam and told her that she couldn't work those streets unless she gave him some pussy.

"No thank you," She told him then went and told Kevin what had happened.

"Don't trip; we can just keep it moving because if you fuck one you'll have to fuck them all." The game is funny like that sometimes.

Down on Lake Worth they ended up running into Pam's old pimp, Tony. They were at the Checkers on Sixth Ave. Tony got out of his car with another guy and walked towards them with a gun.

"Bitch get over here." Tony told Pam.

"I'm not your bitch anymore. I'm with him!"

"Who is this boy?" Tony asked.

"Hold on. I'm a grown ass man. Don't get it fucked up." Kevin warned.

"Bitch don't let me catch you in these streets. Once my bitch, always my hitch."

He then looked at Kevin. "If I see you out on the strip I'ma put a hole in you."

Tony left. Then Pam and Kevin got into the car and followed Tony all the way to the crib. Kevin got his gun from under the seat then got out and shot up Tony's car and yelled, "Who's the boy now?"

Tony got shot three times. Twice in the leg and once in his chest. He started calling Pam's moms crib with threatening messages after the incident. He was saying that he was going to kill Pam and Kevin. Pam's mom called the police on him.

The day after the shooting, Kevin told Alderson about it. Alderson said, "Let's go get that nigga before he finds you."

Kevin and his brother went looking for Tony but didn't find him. They went to Indian town to see Tony's car. He'd gotten the bullet holes fixed. Kevin and his brother shot the car up again and left.

Pam and Kevin then went to the ATL to chill with Kevin's god-brother Larry. While there Pam went out tricking with this Arab for a few hundred dollars. While he was hitting her from the back she somehow lifted fourteen thousand dollars off of him. When she got back she turned it all in to Kevin.

"It's time to go," He told her. "Because we do not know these people."

They made it down to Orlando and chilled at the truck stop. Then got a two bedroom for her to trick out of. She saw two black guys who wanted to trick with her. So she brought them to the room in front of Kevin. Pam would always use condoms to suck dick. It wasn't a problem for either party.

Two days later Pam tricked with this white guy in the back of his truck. She ended up stealing five thousand dollars along with his wallet before leaving. The white guy was mad and crazy as hell when he noticed it. He came back to her room trying to kick the door in yelling, "Bitch I want my money."

"Don't say shit until he leaves," Kevin whispered to Pam.

After a while the guy left. And they did so as well. With all of his money.

The couple headed back to Palm Beach. The day after they got back Pam broke some news to Kevin.

"I'm pregnant," She told him

There wasn't much for him to do about it though because the day after that he got arrested. While on lockdown, Pam gave birth to Kevin's baby girl. Pam's mother kept the baby for a while. And she ended up getting arrested for the robbery she'd committed. But the guy didn't appear in court so she caught a break. Kevin was sentenced to two and a half years for extortion.

Chapter 10

After Kevin got out of prison he bought himself a brown Jaguar. Then drove up and down Broadway thinking about getting himself some whores.

As he was coming from the store he met this one hoe named Jessica. She was 5'6", one hundred and fifty pounds with hazel eyes.

"Can I have a few dollars?" She asked him.

"I'm Big Poppa." Kevin introduced himself.

"When you gon' take me for a ride?"

"Let's go." He told her and ended up at a hotel.

Jessica took a shower while he went to the Flea Market to get some clothes. When he got back Jessica was ass naked on the bed, waiting. Not to try on the clothes he'd bought for her. She wanted to fit him inside of her. Poppa took his clothes off, laid her back and fucked the shit out of her. Jessica's pussy was so wet he got turned on to the third degree. He bent her over doggy-style and went to work on that fat, wet pussy. Jessica got up and took his dick into her wet, warm mouth. Deep-throating him until he came down her throat. After he nutted, Jessica got his dick back hard and road him like a champ.

"Daddy your dick is big as hell. I love this shit."

Big Poppa laid Jessica on her back and pinned her legs back and went to work on that fat, wet pussy. She began cumming so much that it started to run down her asshole. He pulled out and went right into her tight ass. Until he came.

"You with somebody?"

"No."

"Well I need a bitch who is going to get this money."

"Well, I'm that bitch. I'm getting in the shower then getting dressed." When she did that she told Big Poppa, "I'm ready to go."

"Where to."

"I can start where you met me at. On thirteenth avenue. Broadway."

Big Poppa and Jessica drove all the way back to drop her off. Poppa drove to his boy's crib and picked him up to have him drive for him. He and Will ended up at Snookie's bar on Eighth Street. Then went across the street to eat some jumbo shrimp.

He scanned the bar to see this old trick named Michelle. She ran up to see saying, "Big Poppa, it's so good to see you and that you're back home."

"Girl what you doing over this way?"

The O G Pimp From West Palm Beach, Part I

"Well Poppa I still had to make my money, feel me?"

"You hungry?"

"Not for no food. I'm hungry for money."

Poppa, Michelle and Will left to go back to the room. While on the way, Poppa started to tell Michelle about Jessica.

"If you're going to be my hoe I don't want you fuckin' with no black Johns. I mean it. None!"

Back on Belvedere Ave. at the KFC, Poppa ran into the restroom. When he came out Will was talking to this hoe by the car. She turned around and saw Poppa.

She told him, "I know you. I wanna ride with y'all."

"No thanks," Poppa replied. "Let's ride Will."

They went back to the Schooly Inn motel room. Before they got in Poppa saw the curtains move. It was Jessica.

She was happy to see them. Poppa brought her food to her. "Look under the pillow," She told him.

He looked under the pillow to see four hundred dollars. Jessica saw Michelle and gave her a hug and a kiss.

"Damn, I'd love to fuck you girl. You thick." Michelle told her.

"I like her Daddy," Jessica smiled. Then went and laid across the bed. "It's two guys across the walkway who wants to party with me."

"Call 'em and tell 'em your man's back and would like to meet them."

She did so. And the two men came over and knocked on the door. Will got up and sat in the chair with his gun in his lap. Poppa opened the door to let them in.

Jessica walked over. One of them handed her a few hundred dollars that she gave to Poppa before walking out.

"Call as soon as you get there. Just leave the phone off the hook so I can hear what's going on."

"Okay," Jessica said as she left.

She did as she was told and Poppa listened to hear, "Damn your body is bad as hell." Jessica started sexing with her dates.

Michelle walked out to return soon with two hundred dollars from her John. She gave it to Poppa and got into the shower. After taking it he put the phone back to his ear to hear that shit was going good.

"Let me go wash off real fast," Poppa heard Jessica say.

After she came out of the bathroom the two men asked her, "Why don't you come with us?

The O G Pimp From West Palm Beach, Part I

We'll take care of you. We'll give you a car, a crib and some money."

"No, I'm not going to leave my man." Poppa heard.

"Will, let's go get Jessica," He said.

They both jumped up and headed out the door. And so was she. She came over to Poppa and Will and walked into the room. Michelle was getting out of the shower, naked. Jessica gave Poppa three hundred dollars and sat on the bed.

"Take the Jag and go see your wife," Poppa told Will.

Jessica then went and got in the shower. When she returned Poppa told both the naked ladies to get into the bed. Jessica and Michelle laid in the bed and watched Poppa take his clothes off to join.

Jessica and Michelle started kissing each other. Then Jessica sat on Poppa's face while Michelle climbed on top to ride his dick. After a few minutes the girls switched positions and went to work on Poppa. As he grabbed the ass and tittles of Michelle, Jessica deep- throated him unconsciously. After he came, Poppa made Michelle eat Jessica's pussy while he hit Jessica from the back. He fucked her so deep and hard that she started to cum everywhere. After the next switch Poppa fucked Michelle in the ass until he came again. Then he laid back and watched them go at each other. The more Jessica finger fucked and licked Michelle's pussy the more she came. Michelle started eating Jessica's pussy and sticking her tongue in and out of her ass. Jessica came so much that Michelle almost choked from her cum.

Will came back at about three a.m. but Poppa just told him to come back by eight in the morning. Then went back to sleep. At about six o'clock Jessica and Michelle got up to hit Broadway. Michelle came back at 9:30 and Will let her in. She gave Poppa three hundred dollars then took a shower. Poppa and Will was smoking weed when they heard a banging on the door. They jumped up to find Jessica out of breath.

"Two black guys are following me outside." Poppa and Will went outside and flagged the car down. They came back.

"Why y'all following my bitch?" Poppa asked.

"Oh that's your bitch?" One guy asked.

"Yeah!"

"So what you her pimp or some shit?"

"No, that's just my bitch."

Four cops jumped out with guns and said that they were the police. The officers took Poppa and Will down to the station. After a few hours they were released.

They ended up having to move to another motel called Motel 6, on Bluehair Ave. Poppa got

The O G Pimp From West Palm Beach, Part I

double-joined rooms. He dropped Jessica off at the Motel 8 to meet her trick. Then went back to the room to see if Michelle was ready. Before they could make another move, Jessica had hurried back and told Poppa, "I just robbed my trick for sixty-five hundred dollars."

"Everybody pack your shit and be ready to move in a few days."

The following morning at about 4:00 the police were banging at the door. Big Poppa opened the door like he had nothing to hide. The cops grabbed Jessica and took her outside to the car to see if the man she robbed could identify her. Before she was placed in a line-up she'd taken off her wig and make-up. The guy didn't notice her.

"I don't see her," The guy told the cops.

They let her go and she left. But one of the officers came back to try his hand at Jessica because she was bad as hell.

Poppa said, "No cops." So he left.

While eating at Denny's the next day Poppa and Will noticed the same officer walking towards them.

The officer said, "Look, we can help each other out."

He turned to Poppa and said, "I know what you're doing. Let's say that your girls get into trouble. I can get them out."

"So what do you want?" Poppa asked the police officer.

"Well, I like Jessica so much that I will even pay her."

"Look, my girls don't do police. But I will keep that in mind."

"I respect that." The Officer said and got up to leave.

When Poppa got back he moved to the Mariana and stayed in an apartment. After about two weeks Jessica and Michelle ended up getting caught in a police sting for the tricks. They got released the next night and went back to meet Big Poppa.

Standing on the corner was some guy who had got out of his car and smacked Michelle to the ground. Jessica didn't know what was going on.

"Bitch you owe me!" The guy said.

Big Poppa gave Michelle the money to pay the man for a twenty dollar roc' after explaining what happened on their way to meet him.

Big Poppa told the guy, "This my hoe now. So don't fuck with her or give her shit from now on." Then walked off.

Chapter 11

Papa went back to the apartment with Michelle. Jessica had left a note on the table saying that she had gone on a date. The guy next door came by to tell Poppa that Jessica said she left in a black B.M.W. with some white guys and would be back later.

Then he turned his attention to Michelle. "Didn't I tell you to stop getting drugs from other people and that I had it for you. If you don't start listening I'm gon' smack your ass down."

"Alright," She agreed as she laid across the bed. He got ready to fuck her but heard a knock on the door. It was his taxi driver.

"A guy I picked up from the airport is looking for a date."

Papa turned to Michelle and told her, "Get up and go with Patch, the taxi driver to meet this trick."

"He has lots of money and is cool people too," Patch told Papa about the John.

"Okay, call me if you need me."

Hours passed and still no word from Jessica. Papa started to get worried. He called Will. "Come take a ride up and down Broadway with me to see if we see Jessica."

"I'm on my way now, Boss."

As they drove down Broadway Papa spotted the oldest trick around. Old Head Maggie. Papa got out with Will and asked Maggie about Jessica.

"Yeah, I saw her in a black B.M.W. with four white guys. She was looking for another girl to go with her but she just left by herself."

Papa and Will went back to the room. Six more hours went by. It was twelve o'clock and still no Jessica. He started calling the hospitals, jail, friends and police. The taxi driver dropped Michelle off in the midst of everything and she placed one thousand dollars in Big Papa's hand and went to take a shower.

The next morning Jessica showed up and told Papa that the four white guys held her against her will.

"They raped me over and over and took the money back. They were young and used me as a sex slave," She cried. "I didn't cry or try to fight them. I just took whatever came. What really has me mad is that I don't have any money for you."

The O G Pimp From West Palm Beach, Part I

"I'm just glad you're alright." Papa consoled. "I was really worried about you. We looked all over for your ass."

Will and Papa begin discussing a way to get back at these pussies to let them know that they fucked with the wrong bitch.

"I know the license plate number," Jessica told them. She wrote it down and handed it to Papa. Then headed for the shower.

Papa then called that officer who was trying to fuck Jessica and told him, "Run this plate number and get me a telephone number and address."

He wrote down the information then hung up. Papa, Will, Michelle and Jessica then drove to the address to look around.

"There's the car and that's the house," Jessica revealed.

They went back to the spot and Papa called up the Posse from Miami. One female named Angel and three goons; Pee-Wee, Charles and Big John. They popped up about four hours later. Papa explained the situation to them. The Posse was cut-throat. They did the unthinkable to whoever and whenever. Even if it meant using their own bodies to torture you, they would. They all took a ride to show them the layout of Palm Beach Garden. Then they drove back to Riviera.

The next day, Papa went and got a van and laid low until dark fell. Then dressed in all black with vests and strapped up with guns. Will always had his two favorite guns. A nine millimeter and a .357 Super. The windows in the van were tented. Jessica drove. This was the part of Jessica that I wasn't used to seeing. It made me wonder where exactly did she pick this up at. Or was it what I hoped it was and that's instinct.

Once she saw the black B.M.W. she drove into the drive-way and parked behind it. She got out and walked up to the door and knocked. Then she walked back to the van. One of the boys in the house saw Jessica and ran outside. That's when he saw the posse. The posse grabbed him and walked him back to the door and into the house.

Big John grabbed the other white guy and Papa went right over to the mother, and smacked her down. Angel, Michael and Jessica took out all the phone cords. This was 1977, and phone cords were the only form of a phone besides a pay phone. Jessica grabbed the mother's hair and placed a gun to her head while the house got checked.

"Is it anybody else in the house?" Papa asked.

"No!" They said.

"It's clear," Will said as he walked from around the corner.

The O G Pimp From West Palm Beach, Part I

"Is that your car outside?" Papa asked the mother.

"Yes," She replied. "And I'm Katy. These are my sons. "What is it that you want from us?" Katy asked as if she didn't know.

Papa looked at her and said, "You! I want you."

Then walked up to her and slapped the shit out of her.

"Don't fuckin' hit my mother," The young guy named Tim said. Then the posse just started beating the hell out of them.

Papa told Katy, "Look, your sons took my girl to this house in that car and raped her all day and night."

"I was out of town and left the car with them. I just got back in town. What can I do to make this right?"

Then looked at her sons and asked, "Did you do this?" "No, we were just having fun." Tim answered.

Papa pulled his dick out and told Katy, "Suck it!"

She said, "No!"

"Will, check this bitch." Papa pointed.

Will pulled out his .357 Super and put it into her mouth. "Uuummh!" She screamed with the gun in her mouth. "Okay. Okay." Then took Papa's dick into her mouth.

"You'd make a good whore." Papa told her. She sucked faster and faster. "Bitch make me cum so you can swallow drop after drop."

After they finished, Angel put her gun into Katy's mouth and told the other son to, "Suck his dick." She pointed towards Pee-wee. The boy started to cry and Pee-wee walked up to him with his dick out and put it in his mouth, while Tim watched.

Charles walked up to Tim and made him suck his dick. "Damn, you doin' this shit like you like it and done it before. Fuckin' homo, you punk-ass bitch muthafucka."

"Watch this," Papa said. "Take your fuckin' clothes off." He told Katy.

"Please, not this. Not in front of my boys. I'll give you whatever you want."

"Check this bitch, Will."

Will smacked her so hard and fast she damn near fell out.

Jessica put a pistol to her head and said, "Let me rock-a-bye baby this bitch like in New Jack City. Now get naked and get on the floor."

"Damn I'd like to hit that shit!" Big John exclaimed.

"Pull your dick out John," Jessica said to him.

"Suck it!" She demanded Katy.

The O G Pimp From West Palm Beach, Part I

John walked over while pulling his dick out and stuck it into Katy's mouth. She started sucking it then stopped and said, "I got money. Lots of it. I have sixty thousand in my safe. Please don't do this."

"Where is the money?" Papa asked.

"In my bedroom."

"Hold up John, let's go get this money."

Chapter 12

As she was being escorted towards the room Katy asked her sons, "See what having a good time has done to us? You should have never raped that girl." She went to the picture on the wall in her bedroom and removed it. She opened the safe and started removing all of the money and placing it on the bed.

"I want that too," Papa said of the jewelry when he saw it. "This is going to keep y'all alive. Because I was going to kill everybody in here."

"The jewelry belongs to my family. But I have more money in the bank."

"How much?"

"Over one hundred thousand."

"Bring that bitch out here so Big John can fuck the shit out of her like they did me," Jessica ran in and said.

Katy came back out of the room and John put his dick back into her mouth. Then he bent her over and fucked her doggy-style while she screamed. Then he took his dick out of her pussy and fucked her in the ass hard as hell until she started crying and bleeding. Then he put his dick back in her mouth and nutted in it.

"Stop hurting my mother, stop," One of the boys yelled.

Charles grabbed the son and pushed him down on the floor. Then started beating him in the face. Charles grabbed his handcuffs, forced the boy on his stomach and cuffed him. Charles fucked him in the ass fast and hard. The boy started bleeding and crying.

"How does that shit feel you little fuck," Jessica asked.

Charles then grabbed the other boy and he tried to put up a fight. Katy still screamed as John dug off into her. Charles then handcuffed and fucked the shit out of the other boy. He didn't cry or bleed because the gay ass fuckin' homo actually liked the shit.

"How do you like that motherfucker," Jessica yelled. John pulled his dick out of the mother and came all over her face.

She grabbed a sheet to cover up and asked Papa, "Please tell him to stop and let my son come closer to me."

Charles got mad and took the handcuffs off. Then flipped the boy on his back, put him in the 'buck' and fucked him like a bitch. "You like this shit don't you?"

The O G Pimp From West Palm Beach, Part I

Charles talked shit to the boy. He stayed quiet so Charles just fucked him faster and harder. Then the son got off all over Charles' stomach. "What the fuck! You faggot. Bitch you came on me," Charles said and commenced to beat his ass.

"Are you gay?" Pee-wee walked up to the boy and asked.

"Yeah." He answered.

"Where are the guns?" Papa asked. The boys had separate rooms.

"Under his bed."

"Under the mattress." The boys said one after the other.

Papa went to get the guns. He brought them back only to see that they were fake.

"I need the addresses of the other two friends who were with y'all." Papa told the boys after beating them with the fake guns.

One of the boys wrote the phone numbers and addresses down.

"If it's not right, we will be back to kill all of you. And don't call them either. Now take this as a lesson in your life. Don't rape women. And it's not having fun. Never under-estimate anybody," Papa explained to the boys like only an authoritative or father figure could.

"I'm very sorry," One of the boys apologized to Jessica.

"Fuck you. I should kill you right now," Jessica spat.

Papa grabbed her and told her, "Let's go."

"Please, can I at least buy the jewelry back?" Katy asked.

"I will be contacting you soon." Papa answered.

Jessica went out to start the van. Two of the Posse went out the front door and two came out the side. They got in and drove off.

The crew pulled into the Lake Worth Motel and went in to go clean up and change clothes. Papa blocked his number and called the mother right away.

"I want half a million for the jewelry back."

"I don't have that much but I'm damn near close. It's going to take some time because I have to sell my real estate. I can have a large sum of it tomorrow."

"I'll call you back," Papa said and hung up.

The crew loaded back up in the van and drove to Singer Island and checked into the Best Western. The beds were big and they had a lot of room. Will took the van to his friend's house and jumped into his F-350. Will came back in to chill while showers got took and weed got smoked. The next day, Papa split the money with the posse.

Chapter 13

Papa left and went down to E-Zee to get a few phones and beepers for the girls. Papa called Katy and asked her, "Do you have the money for the jewelry"

"Yeah, I have a large sum for you."

"I'm not coming, I'm sending someone. If they don't make it back I will kill you and your sons."

"I can assure you that everything will go as planned."

"Put the money in a brown paper bag and staple it. I'm sending a Rolex and chain until you get the rest. Come to the Super Eight motel behind Denny's in one hour. A girl will be driving a snow white car. No questions, a bag for a bag." Papa sent Michelle to get the money for the jewelry.

Angel followed Katy back to her house but she didn't go home. She went to another house. Angel called Papa and told him the street address.

Papa called Katy and asked her, "Who lives at the address you're at?"

Katy panicked, "How did you know where I was? Someone followed me? Please, this is my aunt's house and she doesn't know anything."

"Are you sure. Because we can come and find out."

"Yes, I'm sure."

"We are watching you. So just keep doing the right thing."

"I will. Please hold the jewelry. I just have to sell more real estate." She begged.

The next visit that was paid to Katy was a little different. She'd been begging Papa to come visit her himself. But instead, he sent someone to pick her up, blind-fold her and take her to switch spots before she arrived where he was. She didn't know where she'd ended up when the truck was parked.

"I can't believe it's really you!" The sexy, green-eyed, red head exclaimed as she rushed up to Papa to embrace him.

"Bitch quit the dumb shit and act like you happy to see me." Papa said, and instantly she dropped to her knees and took him into her mouth. Afterwards, Papa told her, "Get rid of them panties." Then proceeded to suck her pussy and lick her ass like she'd never experienced. He eventually pinned her legs back and long stroked her to cum heaven.

The Posse called the airport and got tickets to catch flights to Atlanta to handle some business.

The O G Pimp From West Palm Beach, Part I

Charles drove the guns up while the rest of the crew flew. They were on their way to pay another one of the guys who'd raped Jessica a visit. Charles had the van painted another color before the mission.

Jessica drove in this one also. She found the house, parked and called the guy on the phone, "Hey, could you come outside?"

"Who is this?" He asked.

"You'll see when you come out."

She walked up to the door as he opened it to walk out. He was about 5'9", two hundred and thirty pounds. When she saw him she turned around and started walking back towards the van. That was their sign. Will pulled his gun out and they all went inside. They walked him to the table in front of his parents. Papa walked to the mother and slapped her down. The dad jumped up and Will checked him by slapping the shit out of him with his gun. The son started trying to fight. Will tusseled him to the ground. Jessica walked up to the mother and put a gun into her mouth. Everybody stopped. Papa had the son and dad cuffed and sat on the floor.

"Now, we're here because your son raped my girl," said Papa.

The dad instantly reached over and smacked the shit out

of the son.

"It wasn't my idea, but I did fuck that trick," Tim said.

Charles walked up to the mother and said, "Take your clothes off, bitch."

Pee-wee and Will put their guns up to the son and dad. Then Angel hit the mom on the side of the head with her blackjack.

"Fuck it; I'm not taking shit off. So you can just kill me." The mom said. She was at least three hundred pounds or more.

John went up to her and wrestled her down and stripped her clothes off. John punched her in the stomach and ribs; she lost her breath and fell to the ground. John made her suck his dick right in front of the father and son. He started fucking her too, while Tim and his dad begged John to stop.

"You fuckin' whore," John said as he fucked her.

"How do you like that," Jessica asked Tim.

Dad tried to get up but he was too big and slow. John fucked the mom faster and faster as he saw her pussy get wetter. The father and son were separated. Then a .357 was pulled and placed in the mother's mouth. John went over and kicked Tim in the stomach. Then made him suck his dick.

Jessica walked over to Tim and told him, "You look like you fucked with the wrong bitch."

The O G Pimp From West Palm Beach, Part I

Pee-wee had his knee in dad's back with the blackjack pulling his head up by the neck, making him watch his son give head. Dad burst out crying, "Stop, stop. What do you guys want?"

Pee-wee went over to Tim and made him suck his dick too. Before he and John came he told Tim to "swallow every drop."

"You want to end this now and get it over with or take it to the next level?" Papa asked.

"End it. What will it take?" Mom asked.

"How much money do you have?" Papa asked.

"Well, most of our money is in real estate, not cash."

"I have money," The son said.

"Don't lie to them," Tim's mother told him.

"I've been saving for a long time. And while y'all were on vacation I had a safe put into my room."

Pee-wee took the son to his room. He returned with seventy-four thousand dollars.

Papa took the money, "The best thing for you to do is to let this go. If you don't we'll be back to kill everybody in the house."

"Don't warn Joe either," Jessica told Tim, referring to the information of the last guy who raped her that he'd given her.

They walked out and left.

"Joe is at home right now," Tim said as they walked out.

They arrived at Joe's house near Palm Beach Garden's school. Jessica didn't go to the door for this one. Angel did. The father answered the door then came outside. Peewee jumped out with his gun then walked him back inside along with Angel. Angel opened the garage once she got in and Papa drove in.

Inside sitting was Mom, dad, Joe and the daughter visiting from college. Papa walked up to Joe and slapped him down. Papa then explained what their son had done.

"That still doesn't give you the right to come into our house the way you did."

"Will, check that nigga." Papa commanded.

Will slapped him in his face with his gun. John started beating on the daughter and making her take off her clothes. The daughter screamed, "Mommy, daddy, do something." To no avail. They had guns to their heads.

John started fucking the shit out of her. Angel held a gun on the mom while Joe and the dad begged them to stop.

"Shut the fuck up," Papa yelled.

"Please stop, she's a virgin," The mother plead.

"Not anymore," Papa told her.

The O G Pimp From West Palm Beach, Part I

After John pulled out, blood ran down the girl's leg from her pussy. John took his bloody dick and put it up to her mouth. "Suck it."

Pee-wee grabbed the mother and threw her down and ripped off her dress. She begged him, "Please, don't do this in front of my kids. Please don't do this to me, please." Pee-wee got on top of her and started fucking.

When John finished getting his dick sucked he took it out of her mouth and started fucking the mom. He pulled out after a few minutes and went straight into her ass. Then into her mouth. Dad tried to help but couldn't do much on his stomach, handcuffed. Charles was holding him down as the daughter sat in a corner with a pillow between her legs, crying. Jessica walked up and slapped the shit out of her, then laid on the couch and told her to, "Eat my pussy bitch." She complied.

Papa walked over to Joe and asked him, "Was it worth it?"

"No, we were just drinking. I'm sorry."

While the daughter was sucking Jessica's pussy, Charles came up behind her and fucked her doggy-style.

She screamed, "It hurts, it hurts." As Charles went deeper into her.

"I was a virgin, I was a virgin," She said as he went faster.

Jessica pulled her head down into her pussy to shut her up. Charles pulled his dick out of her pussy and went into her ass. Fast and hard until her ass started to bleed. Then went back into her pussy. Charles got up and went over to Joe and made him suck his dick. "You better not drop a drip or I will kill you myself."

Big John laid on the couch and made the mom ride his dick until he came. Pee-wee grabbed Joe around the neck and started choking him. Then pushed him to the ground and fucked him in his ass deep and hard. After all this finished, Papa talked to the dad and he gave Papa a large sum of money. Then they all left.

When they got back to the room Papa called Katy. She told him that she had more money. Papa set up a meeting, went to see her and exchanged the jewelry for money. Then he began to treat her like a good whore.

After it was all said and done, all of the families kept everything to themselves. Avoiding further repercussions.

Papa's Quotes

You can't just go out one day and say you're a pimp. Keep it real with yourself. This is a real game that takes a real man who has what it takes. Understand that being a pimp is not a good thing at all. At times, trust me as a pimp; a lot of people don't like you. You must stay on top of your game at all times.

The game came to me; I didn't go to the game. Yes, I like it a lot. But that's all I know. I lived the life. It's me no matter where I go. I tell all my girls, "This game is not for a girl who don't like to fuck and suck. A hoe is a toy you play with." Get into her mind. Teach her how to get money.

I have been in this game for thirty-five years. I live off of the land I sleep on. I'm one of the best. See, guys give this game a black eye by watching it on TV and not knowing a damn thing about being a pimp.

Next here is a little game about renegade hoes...

Part Two: Tina and Kelly

One of Papa's rules is "No renegade hoes." Because he doesn't like them in his business. These types of hoes always try to be in a pimp's business only because they don't have a pimp of their own. They do shit like, see girls on the strip and tell them, "You don't need no pimp. You can keep all the money you make."

And start telling them, "You can have more money by working for yourself," Hating because they are lost. They have nowhere to live. And no steady clientele.

In this game, Big Papa learned one thing. That's "Trust no one but yourself." Always be on top of your shit. And your hoes, at all times. Any girl that was on Big Papa's team was there by choice, not by force. A lot of his hoes chose him, he didn't pick them. Sometimes they found themselves in trouble and called him. Because they felt like Big Papa could get them out of anything at anytime.

Down in West Palm Beach, people just respected Big Papa. And it was not out of fear. He earned his respect by standing up when it was time to stand up. On Broadway in West Palm Beach there were two girls living in the Queen's Lodge who were working the street. Their names were Kelly and Tina. Kelly and Tina didn't have a pimp. They were doing their own thing. Until one day Papa saw them both getting out of his girls' date car. Papa sent a message by one of his girls to let them know to stay out of his business, or else. Papa's girl came back after confronting them and said, "They told me they work for Big Papa."

Later that night, Papa paid them a visit. He had a girl to knock on their door and Kelly answered it. Papa walked in and said, "Why y'all out here using my name? Y'all told me that y'all don't need no pimp."

At that time, Lester was sitting in the car at Queens Lodge. He was one of the tricks. Papa sent one of his girls to bring Lester inside.

"Are these your girls?" He asked Lester.

"Yeah. I've been with them for about two weeks. They told me that they work for you. I thought it was cool." Lester said then exited the room with one of Papa's girls.

"Check them hoes." Papa told Will.

Will slapped Kelly down to the floor. Then did the same to Tina.

"If y'all gon' work Broadway, y'all got to work for me. But I don't need you on Broadway."

The O G Pimp From West Palm Beach

Papa had come to find out that Tina and Kelly had been dating a lot of his clientele. Papa gave them a quota to make every day. They had made money all month with no problems. They thought they'd paved a way.

"Don't get personal with any of your dates." Papa told them.

Kelly began dating this guy named Lee. He was older and his son was a police officer for West Palm Beach. A few weeks had went by and Papa told Kelly and Tina that, "Y'all can leave if you want to."

"No, we're okay with the agreement." They responded.

One day after a date with Lee, Kelly came back with five thousand dollars and two Masonic rings. After she got out of the shower, Papa asked her about the rings and the money.

"It's from a date from out of town. He slipped so I got him."

After drinking and smoking, Kelly took Papa into her mouth, deep-throating him so good that his eyes started to roll into the back of his head as his toes popped. Papa bent Kelly over doggy-style and fucked the shit out of her. After about thirty minutes, Papa slid his dick into her ass and went to work. She started moaning and screaming, "Daddy don't stop. Go harder, faster, deeper." Papa fucked

Kelly so good she just gave in and let him have his way.

Breakfast that morning was sex. Then they got their stuff together and went back down towards Queen's Lodge. They went back to the Motel Six in Riviera Beach and Papa got four rooms. One was for Precious. She was Papa's bottom bitch. Her job was to do shit that no one else would do. She also held shit down while Papa was gone. And kept all the hoes in line with money matters. Precious was Puerto Rican with long black hair. She was really thick with a fat ass and wide hips. She also had a pretty face and a nice set of titties.

"The police have been by looking for you and left a card saying please contact them, and that you could work this out." Precious told him when he walked in later on.

Papa called the number.

"Yes, I'm Lee's son. The older man who's been with Kelly. She took my father's money and rings. I'm not worried about the money, but the rings mean a lot to our family."

"Well, I have the rings and don't have a problem giving them back."

"You don't know how much this means to me." He told Papa. "My father should know better than to take a whore back to his condo."

The O G Pimp From West Palm Beach

The two men met and Papa gave the rings back to the son. The cop then gave Papa a card with a personal number on it and told him, "If you ever get into a jam, use this number."

Papa went into the room and told Precious to, "Go get Kelly," while Tina was still on her date.

When Precious brought Kelly back he slapped her down on site. Then beat her ass. "You stole these fuckin' rings and put heat on me bitch. The cops just left here. Now you need to go back down to Palm Beach and find somewhere else to work. If I see you we will have a problem."

Tina walked in to see Kelly beat up and bruised. "What happened?" She asked.

"Let's roll." Precious came in and told the girls. She took Kelly and Tina hack to the queen's Lodge and left them.

Two hours later, Papa got a call from Lee telling him, "I'm in love with Kelly and I really need to see her. I don't care about the money. Just let me be with her."

A few days later, Lee's son Roy called telling Papa "I need to see you."

When they met Roy asked Papa to, "Please keep Kelly away from my father."

"Look, I told Kelly not to be around Lee anymore."

"I went to my father's condo to see her asleep in his bed." Roy cut in. "I told her to leave but my father told me not to tell him who can come and go in his home. Then he put me out. So I left."

Papa nodded at Lee's statement.

"I'll take care of it." He told Roy.

Two weeks had went by since Papa's conversation with Roy. He stumbled upon Kelly at the Flea Market in a B.M.W. She was up on 45th shopping with the old man's credit card.

He waited until she stepped off into the bathroom then told two of his goons, "Go check her ass, hard."

They went in right behind her and beat the shit out of her. Real bad. They took the B.M.W. and the credit card. Then told her, "Stay away from Lee or else." After cutting her hair and knocking out a few teeth, they thought she'd gotten the picture. She was also with a black eye and a few broken ribs.

That same night Papa got a call from Lee saying, "No matter what happens, Kelly and I are going to be together."

Lee ended up moving out of his condo to Melbend County with Kelly where he bought another condo. Kelly fell in love with Lee because she knew he cared about her. So she stayed with him. Lee and Kelly ended up getting married. He was sixty-seven. She was only twenty-three.

The O G Pimp From West Palm Beach

Two months after the wedding, Lee had a heart attack and died. Lee left Kelly with millions of dollars in assets. Roy was upset to the fullest. Because he wasn't left with anything. Kelly turned out to be one rich bitch after all.

Pretty Ricky

Pretty Ricky, another pimp pulled up in his B.M.W. at the Dollar Room motel and got a few rooms. A few hours had went by and he had his hoes on the strip getting all of Big Papa's clientele. He had two black girls and three white girls on the stroll. He even began to follow some of Big Papa's hoes around to see what he could do with them.

One of Papa's girls came back to let him and Will know what was going on. Then another came in and told him, "I know where Pretty Ricky's room is."

Papa and Will paid the pimp a visit. They waited for one of the girls to leave out before walking in with three pistols pointed. But Ricky and his man had theirs drawn also as if they were waiting for them.

"What's up? Do we have a problem?" Pretty Ricky asked.

"You stepping on my toes, man." Papa told him. "Those are my hoes you been following around."

"Look, where I'm from in Memphis, it's open game." Ricky bit back. "I can talk to whoever, whenever I get ready to."

"Look, y'all ain't takin' shit over. And because y'all got guns, don't mean shit. You better be gone by the time I get back or else." Papa threatened as he and Will left to go back to the room.

That same night, Pretty Ricky and his man were at the store when Will saw his B.M.W. and told Papa. So Papa sent his two goons to go break out the windows and set the car on fire. Then Papa had his two goons to pose as Johns for two of Pretty Ricky's white hoes. The goons held the white hoes in a room for a few days for Papa.

The hoes ended up telling Papa, "We don't want to be with Pretty Ricky. We were forced to trick for him," They explained.

"Well I want y'all to go to another area until I finish with him."

Papa drove by the Dollar Motel to see fire trucks and Pretty Ricky talking to the cops. Then he watched as two of Pretty Ricky's blacks girls got into a cab with two black guys and left. Papa went back to the room after that.

And one of the white girls told Papa, "I want to go back home and get away from tricking."

"Will, get her a bus ticket and take her to the bus station." He said instantly.

The O G Pimp From West Palm Beach, Part I

"We want to work for you," One of the white girls spoke for the other two.

Papa's phone rang. It was the manager from the Arrow Motel. "The construction crew is back looking for you and the girls."

"Pack up y'alls stuff. We're headed to Orlando."

<u>Orlando, Florida</u>

"I want y'all to dye your hair," Papa told the girls.

Pam and Cindy dyed their hair from black to blonde. Precious and Princess went from blonde to black. What didn't change though was Precious' apt to carry a gun. She was a licensed carrier; she always carried her gun on her. Kato, Will and Papa followed the girls. Precious pulled into a truck stop to use the restroom. Papa looked around and saw about fifteen truckers. To him, they all looked like huge dollar signs.

The girls stepped out in short skirts and high heels to get the truckers' attention. All four girls went to work right there on the spot for about an hour. They were coming out of the trucks and restrooms left and right. Papa, Will and Kato went into the truck stop to get them something to eat. Papa went into the restroom to see Precious on her knees sucking this white guys dick who he'd just seen sitting with his family. Precious stopped and gave Papa three hundred dollars, then bent over to let her trick fuck her doggy-style. Papa left out of the restroom, went and got his food then went to the van with Will and Kato.

Pam and Princess came back to the van with their money and gave it to Papa. Then Precious followed with more money as well. They waited on Cindy. She was in the back of a truck getting fucked in all three holes. She rode a guy while another fucked her in the ass. She was deep-throating the third guy. After a few minutes they tried to rotate.

"Maybe next time guys. I've got to go, it was fun," She said as she pocketed her two thousand dollars. One of them just held her head back with her hair as they all came on her face and in her mouth. Then put her out.

Papa watched Cindy run to the restroom to wash up a little. Then brought Papa the two thousand dollars.

"That's my girl," He told her. "Now let's go." He told the crew.

They arrived in Orlando's Orange Blossom Trail. Also known as O.B.T. Then checked into the Arrow Motel. All of the girls got their own rooms with two beds in them.

The O G Pimp From West Palm Beach, Part I

"Kato, go pick up Kim," Papa said referring to one of the trail blazers. He needed to see what had changed since he was last there.

Kato went to O.B.T. to pick Kim up as a date. He picked her up and went back to the room where Big Papa was.

"Oh shit, Big Papa hey Daddy."

"How is shit?" Papa asked Kim.

"Look O-B-T is the stroll for all hoes. There are a lot of strip clubs and restaurants. So it stays busy all night long."

The girls put on their swim wear and hit the pool. About five truck drivers watched them from the restaurant. They all got up to go meet the girls. But before they even reached them the girls asked, "Are y'all looking for dates."

"Yeah." One of the truckers answered.

The truckers had rooms at the same motel, so business was good. After Papa watched the girls go into the rooms with them, he went next door to order three chickens from Ms. Peggy and came back. Precious had come right back to the room with nine hundred dollars.

"They want to pay more to keep us over for the barbeque," She told Papa.

The truckers paid the manager for the pool to be closed off and paid Papa his as well. After it started to get dark one of the men went in to call Papa.

"Do you mind if we take some naked pictures of the girls?"

"Yes, I don't want y'all to do that."

Princess came in with Sandy and gave Papa five hundred dollars apiece. Then went back to work. Pam came back with seven hundred dollars and told him, "It's not over. I'll be right back daddy."

A few hours later all the girls came back with so much food that Kato and Will had to help bring it all in. The girls then went back to chill with the truckers for a few more hours until Papa called and told them, "It's time to leave."

The girls got their last few tricks in before returning with more money for Papa. They showered and got ready for the town; because it was Friday and the town needed to know that they were there.

Kato and Papa walked around the rooms to see the girls had met a construction crew who wanted dates as well. It was better this way for the girls because this way they could keep an eye on each other. They came back with no less than one thousand dollars apiece.

"Put a hit of crack on the pipe and lay down so I can eat your pussy," A John told Cindy in their room.

The O G Pimp From West Palm Beach, Part I

She did and had a blast. But the guy ran out of money within two hours. So he left and returned with three thousand dollars. He bought more crack and pussy from Cindy. Pam hadn't answered her door in a few hours. Or hadn't called in. So precious went and tried to get into the room but couldn't.

"I need you to open a door for me," Papa went and told the manager.

He did so, and Papa pushed the door open to see Pam riding her date. Papa closed the door back and went to the room. A few minutes later, Pam came in with five hundred dollars and gave it to Papa.

"Will, check this bitch, man. She don't seem to understand the rules of checking in every hour on the hour." Will checked her real good. "Now call your date and tell him you're not coming back." She did so. "Now get in the shower and go hit O-B-T." Papa commanded her. She gave Papa a fucked up look he didn't like. "Will, check this bitch again." Will slapped Pam open handed down to the floor. "I want four hundred dollars from you within an hour." He told Pam.

Pam left the room mad as hell. And returned an hour later fifty dollars short. Papa called her into the room and asked her, "What's the problem?"

"I have three hundred and fifty dollars."

"Will, check this hard headed bitch again because I said four hundred dollars. Not three fifty."

After Will fucked her up Papa told her, "Change clothes and get back out on the strip. This time bring me all of my money."

On her way out Pam got stopped by four black guys trying to date her. She went to make a phone call.

"Do you mind if I go on a date with four black guys?" She asked Papa.

"Have them meet me first."

After meeting with Papa they gave him two hundred dollars each and told him. "Two of us for a hour, then the next two for a hour."

"That's straight." Papa agreed.

The party left and went into the room.

Cindy called and told Papa, "My date is tweeking out. He needs some more crack. He wants me to take his car and credit card and go get more money."

"Check with me when you get back."

Cindy came back after getting three thousand dollars out of the trick's account and showed Papa the receipt. There was sixty-four thousand in his account. The trick wanted two more girls to freak with. Then gave Papa his credit card. Papa sent Precious and Princess over to meet him. They got

The O G Pimp From West Palm Beach, Part I

ass naked and laid across the bed. Cindy was on the phone with Papa.

"Why do I hear all the water running?"

"He said he wants it to sound like it's raining." Cindy explained to Papa.

"Put him on the phone." Papa told Cindy.

"How much money can you take out at one time?" Papa asked once the John got on the phone.

"There's no limit."

"Bet."

Precious and Princess laid there licking each other's pussy while the trick watched. After Precious kissed Princess down she went to sucking on her titties. After a few moans and more licks Precious went back down to eat out Princess's pussy. She fucked her with her tongue and face. Princess came all over the place but Precious wasn't done yet. She turned her over and licked her asshole until she came again. Princess was so horny after that she just dove into Precious with lust-filled eyes. Princess ate her so good that she came herself. Then started pushing her finger into Precious's ass while licking her clit. Precious is a hard cummer. And she exploded on Princess's face. Tim laid the pipe down and laid on the bed so that Precious could sit on his face. Princess sat on his dick and they both began to grind on him. Cindy stayed on the other bed getting high and playing with herself

"Eat her pussy while I fuck you from the back." Tim told Precious while pointing at Princess.

After a few minutes, they switched. He fucked Princess in the ass while she ate Precious out. All three of them soon came like waterfalls. After they all got done, they showered and dressed.

"You can take out five thousand." Tim called and told Papa.

Papa came over and told Precious to go with Princess to get the money. Cindy stayed with Tim while he smoked more crack. Papa went back to the room to let Will and Kato know what was going on. The girls arrived with five thousand dollars and gave it to Papa.

He called Cindy on the phone, "Come on back to the room."

He then sent Pam to chill with Tim and told her, "Call back when you get there."

When Cindy walked in he told her to, "Get your clothes, take a shower and come to the back room to see me."

Cindy did as she was told. She and Papa had a few drinks and talked about Tim and his money. Afterwards, he told her to, "Get naked."

He started eating her pussy while she deep-throated him in the sixty-nine position. Then Papa bent her over doggy—style and, beating the pussy up with long, hard, fast strokes as if showing his

The O G Pimp From West Palm Beach, Part I

appreciation for a job well done with Tim. Cindy moaned louder and louder until she came all over Papa.

"Put it in my ass," She told him.

Papa didn't waste any time. He went deep off into it, pounding away. The more she screamed the more she came. Then Papa pulled out and Cindy took him into her mouth and swallowed every drop.

After cleaning up and showering again, Cindy told Papa, "Tim told me he had stocks and bonds. He also said that he has jewelry inside his truck. He and his dad got into it, but his father still made him come on the job anyway."

Meanwhile, the truckers had called Princess and Precious because they wanted a date before they left. The girls met with the truckers for a "quickie". They were done in less than twenty minutes. They paid the girls two hundred dollars apiece and asked them, "Do ya'll want to come with us."

"No thanks. We have to get back. Bye!" Precious spoke.

Papa went to go get some food and back. Cindy sat back, smoked her weed then ate all her food and some of Papa's too.

Papa's hoes were the ones people stopped for. Take Cindy for example. She was 5'5", one hundred and twenty pounds with hair down to her ass.

Her eyes were deep blue. She was thick, fine with pretty feet. She was always joyful and happy. She was also loyal. She loved hard core sex. The rough stuff, doggy style.

Pam was a short thang; 5'4", one hundred and thirty five pounds, big booty and red-headed. Her eyes were green and she had a nice set of titties. Pam was real stubborn. And loved to fight. She loved to take control in the bed when she could. And also loved to fuck girls. Papa never stuck his dick in Pam. Never.

Precious was Papa's bottom bitch. She was 5'8", one hundred and fifty pounds. She had big titties and long black nipples. She had long, black, thick, silky hair. She was also a Brown belt. Sex was her passion. She loved to please a man. She was extremely loyal and did whatever tricks wanted done.

Princess was about 5'10", one hundred and twenty pounds. She had nice small titties and big pink lips. She was pretty as hell; long haired, cute faced and very soft spoken. She was also very sexual. She enjoyed riding dick more than anything. Princess always watched her man as he came. And always got whatever she wanted.

Precious ended up getting two dates through Kim from O.B.T. Precious went to Papa's room to let him know and to call Ray to set up the date for five hundred apiece.

The O G Pimp From West Palm Beach, Part I

"Can I bring some gin to drink?" He asked. "Yeah sure."

When Ray pulled up with his friend Precious told Princess to, "Come with me."

They went outside to see a candy apple-red Corvette with white inside. It was real clean. While the girls were at the car, Papa put tape recorders inside of both rooms as well as video. Once she got inside the room Precious called Papa and left the phone off the hook. Princess did the same.

Precious and Ray started drinking, touching and then kissing. Precious undid Ray's pants, pulled his dick out and started deep-throating him like the pro that she was. Precious went down to his balls then licked his ass until he came down her throat. Ray flipped her over on her back and ate her pussy while fingering her in the ass. When her pre-cum started to flow, Ray sucked on her clit until she exploded all over his face. Ray climbed on top of her, pinned her legs back and pounded her wet pussy to death. Precious came over and over, again and again. Then he turned her over and fucked her doggy-style hard and deep.

Before he came he pulled out and slid into her ass. He pounded away hard in her ass until he came.

Jerry asked Princess to dance for him.

"Why don't I just fuck you like a whore?"

Jerry took off his clothes and Princess did the same. He started kissing her in the mouth while fingering her pussy as she jacked his dick. Jerry laid Princess down and began to suck her titties and then licked down to her pussy while still fingering her.

"Bend over." Jerry told Princess so that he could eat her pussy and ass from the back. Princess came so hard it overwhelmed her.

She got on her knees and took him into her mouth. Princess sucked Jerry's dick so good that he gave in and came in her mouth. Princess hummed on his balls for a few minutes then got him back hard. She climbed on top of him and rode him until both of them came.

After a few hours the girls got hungry and wanted something to eat.

"We'll give y'all extra money just to chill with us and keep us company." Ray told them.

Princess took the money, took it over to Papa and came back to chill. Jerry poured drinks.

"I'm a pilot. And my money is as long as the flights I take." Jerry told Princess.

Ray handed them both one thousand dollars and said, "We want the both of you to fuck each other before we leave."

The O G Pimp From West Palm Beach, Part I

Precious took the two thousand back to Papa and told him, "He wants us to fuck each other." Then went back.

Princess and Precious took showers then laid on the bed for Ray and Jerry to watch. Princess started sucking Precious' titties while Precious finger fucked her. Then they got into the sixty-nine position and started sucking each other's pussy. Princess got up and bent Precious over to eat her ass and pussy. Precious followed up with the same acts. Princess came all over her face. Precious continued by fingering Princess in the ass and pussy until she came again.

After night fell the girls told Ray and Jerry, "Let's do you." But before they got busy Precious collected four hundred more dollars and took it to Papa. Ray began by fucking Princess doggy-style. And Precious rode Jerry hard. Then Princess turned around and started giving Ray some sloppy head. He enjoyed it while fingering her in her ass. Jerry put Precious in the sixty-nine until she started shaking with cum. It ran into his mouth and down his face. Ray came all over Princess then went right to her ass and pounded away.

"Fuck me hard until I cum." Princess told Ray.

"Go deeper and faster. Make me cum." Precious told
Jerry.

The both of them came; and they all laid there to rest. Papa had the room under control with the cameras. So he knew what went on at all times. Jerry and Ray left while the girls took showers. Then went to go see Papa.

"What did y'all do?" He asked them.

They gave him the run-down. In all honesty. So shit was good.

"When we're out of town, anything goes and all game is fair." Papa told them. "Go to the store and get some gin and sweet & sour mix." They did so.

On the way back Princess saw a Porsche, pulled up next to it and parked. When she got out she saw a money bag in it. She opened the door. The alarm went off and she grabbed the bag.

"Bitch, get in." Precious yelled, and they pulled off with the bag of money. Precious called Papa and told him what had happened and where they were. Will and Papa got into the mini-van and went to where they were. Precious took all of the money out of the bag and put it into her pocket book bag. And dropped the money bag in the dumpster where they were.

Papa told them to, "Get out of the van and take a cab to the bus station." Then he called Kato and told him, "Go get the van and clean it up."

After meeting the girls at the bus station they got into the mini-van and Papa started counting all

The O G Pimp From West Palm Beach, Part I

the money. It was a little over seventeen thousand. Will drove to the Walgreen's to get the girls some dye for their hair. Precious went blonde and Princess turned into a red-head. Papa turned around and asked, "Where is my gin?" The girls laughed.

"Daddy did we do a good job?" Princess asked.
"Yeah."

After making it back to the motel Pam told Papa, "Tim is trying to go back to the bank." Pam then gave Precious the credit card and told her, "Take out five thousand." Then went back to go chill with Tim.

Cindy was still asleep while all of this was going on.

"I'll give you one thousand dollars to give me a golden shower," Tim told Pam. She did. She pissed all over him as he jacked his dick.

Then she came back with the money and gave it to Papa. Papa woke Cindy up and the first thing she did was light up some weed. Papa threw all the money on the bed to show her what she'd missed.

"This is how a hoe is supposed to get money."

"Damn, I wish that could have been me." She said.

"Look, we all work together as a family. When one brings in money, all get credit for it. I want you to go chill with Tim."

Tim had four thousand dollars left. He spent two thousand on crack and one thousand on Cindy to chill with him.

Papa got a knock at the door. It was the owner, Mr. Patel.

"Can you watch over the motel and keep an eye on my wife. I have to leave for a few days and I consider you a good friend. Can you do this for me?"

"Sure."

"Thank you, my friend."

Mr. Patel left for the airport and Papa went back to his room. The next day, Papa went to check up on Mrs. Patel to make sure that everything was cool. He knocked on the door. She said, "Come in."

"I was just checking on you for your husband."

"Okay, thank you." Then there was a beat of silence before she said. "I see the way you look at me." Then kissed Papa on the mouth real hard and sensual.

Papa wasted no time. He pushed her back on the bed and pulled her dress up to reveal a fat, hairy pussy. Papa took off his clothes, pinned her legs back and fucked the shit out of her. He pulled out and told her, "Suck Daddy dick." She did; fast, then slow, and fast again until he came.

The O G Pimp From West Palm Beach, Part I

Papa then bent her over doggy-style and fucked her until she came. Then he stuck it in her ass and pounded away hard, deep and fast. She screamed so loud that Papa began to slap her on the ass to calm her down. "I'm 'bout to cum," He told her. So she turned around and started deep-throating him until he came down her throat. Then they laid down together.

"Am I wrong for having sex with another man if my husband doesn't spend time with me anymore?"

"No, you're not wrong. Just don't fuck anybody else. You can call me anytime for some dick and I won't tell your husband if you don't."

After those hot two hours of bashing Mrs. Patel in Papa went back towards the room and saw a fine ass black woman. None were in his stable at the time. He just had to turn around. He didn't fuck Black women like that but he couldn't resist this temptation. This was one of the prettiest sisters he's ever seen.

"Can I help you with those bags?"

"Sure."

Papa helped her to her room and she asked him, "Would you like something to drink?"

"Yeah."

After retrieving it, she started telling Papa about her problems with her husband.

"I just had to get away for a few days." She explained. After smoking some weed and having a few drinks Papa sat there and listened to her intensely. He didn't come on to her sexually. There was just a lot of conversation going on.

"Baby girl, I have to get back," He told her after a while.

"Well, okay. I guess I will see you soon."

Papa went back to his room. Then heard someone yelling really loud. Will and Papa rushed out to see an old woman yelling, "My grandson can't swim. He's fell into the pool. He's drowning."

Papa jumped into the pool and saved the young boy. He pulled him out and gave him C.P.R. to bring his breathing back. The police came with the ambulance and took a statement. They told Papa, "You did a good job and a great deed by saving this young child's life."

The mother and father came with the grandmother to thank Papa as well. They even tried to give Papa money.

The truckers called and asked Precious, "Can you all come by in a few. We have someone we'd like to introduce you to."

"Yeah," Precious told him. Then called Papa to let him know.

Papa and Will went back to the room and ordered everybody drinks. The truckers pulled up and

The O G Pimp From West Palm Beach, Part I

went right over to the pool area and lit the grill. They brought their two sons as their company. It was one of their birthdays. They gave Papa a large sum of money and told him, "We would like to chill for two days."

"It's cool," Papa told him. "Stay here with the truckers and do as they ask." Papa told all four girls.

The truckers paid for private pool time and closed the gate. Everybody was naked. And for the money that they gave Papa, anything went. Precious took the son whose birthday it was into the pool and started fucking the shit out of him. Then sucked his dick so long that he damn near fell asleep. Getting out of the pool, Princess told him to, "Sit down." And started to give him some deep-throat as well. Then rode his dick until he came. Pam and Cindy took hold of the other son and went to work.

"Fuck me from the back." She told him while she sucked his father's dick.

Pam was getting fucked from the back by the other father until he came. Then she sucked his dick until he got back hard. Then he fucked her in the ass until she came again.

The son didn't have enough strength to hang all night. So they chilled in the pool kissing around with the girls until they were ready.

"Get on your knees and suck my balls then my dick." After a few minutes he told her, "Bend over so that I can stick my tongue in your ass." Precious did as she was told.

Cindy came over so that he could do the same to her. Pam and Ray fucked off to the side. Princess took both the sons and let them fuck her at the same time. One was in her mouth; the other was in her ass.

Two days later, after the session Papa told Will and Kato, "It's time to black—male Ray. He wants to be with the girls, but he loves his wife."

After making copies of the sex tape, Papa sent Precious to give Ray a copy of the tape. "If you give Papa a large sum of money, you won't ever have to worry about hearing anything else about it." Was her message.

Ray met with Papa and told him, "Look, if I do this I want to keep seeing the girls and my wife can't find out about it."

"Agreed." Papa took the money.

"How will I know that it won't happen again?" Ray asked Precious.

"You just have to trust what's going on."

"What about the car, Ray?" Papa asked.

"No. Just take the money. I need to speak with you about something else though. I want to have a child with Cindy."

The O G Pimp From West Palm Beach, Part I

"Hell no." Papa responded.

Later on, Jerry called Papa and told him, "Hey, I want a date with the girls but I don't want Ray to find out. Can we arrange this?"

"Yeah, we can definitely set it up."

Jerry showed, and paid for Cindy. They went into the room. Papa had them on tape. Now he could black mail Jerry as well. Cindy sucked and fucked Jerry to sleep.

Papa got a call from the rental car facility about the van.

"We found it burned from a fire."

"Damn, I didn't know nothing about it. Thank you for letting me know," He played them. He then went into the room with the crew and told them, "Look, it's time to go." They left like a thief in the night.

They ended up in Juno Beach at the Castle Motel. They all got rooms and coupled off so that things would look better. The following day, the girls went to the mall to spend some money and spent it well they did. Precious ended up coming out of one of the stores and making the metal detector go off because of her gun. She had her permit on her so she was escorted back to the car where she put it in the trunk.

When they finished shopping, Papa had a taste for some jumbo shrimp. So they went to eat at a seafood restaurant. There, Papa saw this young, twenty year old pretty thing. She was a real redhead. She had green eyes also and a nice fat ass. Kinda reminded him of Katy. Man, had Katy blown his mind the way she fell for him after the stunt they pulled on the family. Anyway, Papa walked away from Precious and went over to talk to the young cashier.

After coming back to the table, she came to take their order. "My name is Kandy." She told them.

The girls then began to tell Kandy how pretty she is and how attractive she was. Princess sparked a conversation with her. And Cindy joined in. Kandy conversed, laughed and smiled the entire time they gave her attention.

Precious gave her the cell phone number and told her, "Call us. We're having a beach party tonight. You should come."

"Okay, sure. I'll call and get the directions on how to get there." Kandy winked her eye at Papa and walked back to her area.

They all watched her walk back. She had a fat, juicy ass and she slung it everywhere.

Later that night, Papa and the girls waited to see if she would show up. Kandy called and came right over, got cool with the girls and started drinking with Papa. Princess walked out to see Kandy and

The O G Pimp From West Palm Beach, Part I

went right over to her and gave her a hug and a light grab on the ass.

Kandy just smiled and went with the flow. After a few more drinks, Princess started rubbing her down and kissed her on the lips, telling Kandy, "You are so fine and sexy."

Kandy began to kiss Princess back harder and harder. Precious came over to them and kissed Kandy also. Then just pulled a titty out and licked her nipple until she moaned. Cindy and Pam came over and started taking off her pants. The both of them went to work on her pussy. Until she came all over them. Then said, "Big Poppa, I've been waiting on you all night."

"Girls excuse us for a moment," Papa told the rest of the girls.

They left and told Kandy, "We'll be back for you later."

Papa took Kandy to the bed, then laid her down and ate her pussy over and over until she begged him to stop. Then, Kandy got between Papa's legs and sucked his dick like a young girl on a lolly pop. Papa came unusually fast in her mouth. Then got on top of her and pinned her legs back and fucked the shit out of her. He bent her over doggy-style and dug deep off into her good and hard.

"Fuck me in the ass until I can't take it no more." She told Papa.

Papa fucked her so hard and deep that she was surprised herself at how wide her ass spread. He came in her ass then she instantly sucked his balls to get him back hard. And climbed on top of him to ride his dick until she came all over Papa's dick. Then passed out.

Papa and Kandy talked about her life right afterwards.

"I was adopted at ten years old. I always wanted to be a part of something."

"Well, you can be a part of this family. But you got to be down to do whatever."

"I understand what I'm getting into. I'm willing to give it a try. I used to get sexually abused by my foster mother's nephews. I lost my virginity at thirteen years old."

"That's your past. That's not what makes you." Papa told her. "You still have time to get a decent education. And do whatever it is you want. Being a whore is not what it seems." Papa told Kandy as they now strode along the beach.

Then Kandy stopped and told Papa, "I'm grown, my life is what it is. This is what I want to be. I want to be a part of your escort service. I'll do whatever it takes to make that money and make you proud."

Damn, I can't let this fine ass green-eyed red head go to waste. Fuck it.

The O G Pimp From West Palm Beach, Part I

"First is the golden rule. Do what I tell you when I tell you. Don't take orders from no one else unless I tell you to."

Kandy looked at Papa and said, "to be honest, I want to tell you that my foster father has been fucking me for the last three years; I think I like it, I'm not sure."

Bingo! Papa thought, he could blackmail him. "I'll move in with the girls today if you let me."

"Yeah, go ahead and get your shit. Fast. How much

money do you have in the bank?"

"Twelve thousand dollars."

"Ten of that goes into my pocket."

"Fine with me."

After getting her clothes and taking Precious to get the money from the bank they went back to the Castle motel. Candy walked into the room with Papa, took off all of her clothes, got on her knees and gave Papa all the money. "I'm going to be the loyal one for you. I'm your hoe for life." In front of everybody.

Papa placed Kandy on the bed, took his clothes off and fucked the shit out of her while everybody else watched. He talked dirty to her. Then told her, "Your new name is, Baby Girl from now on."

"Yes Daddy," Baby Girl said. Then proceeded to suck the life out of him.

"Will, bring me the camera," He said. Then told everyone else, "Y'all can leave now. Get on the bed and pose for me Baby Girl." He took pictures of her in every position possible. "You got a pretty pussy. I like how you keep your hair trimmed." He told her.

After getting the snapshots of Baby Girl with her in doggy-style, with her legs pinned back behind her head and with her laying on her back Papa posted them on the Internet with a contact number.

Within an hour his phone was ringing non-stop. She picked up the phone and went with the flow. She had plenty of dates lined up real fast. One of the dates came right over. So Papa got them a room and he gave Papa four hundred dollars. Then went to work on Baby Girl.

They finished after about an hour and he left and told a friend; who told a friend. Baby Girl built clientele fast as ever. She went through five or six Johns in a matter of hours. Fucking and sucking like crazy. She brought Papa three thousand dollars.

"Is your body hurting?" He asked her.

"No, I'm fine."

"I want you to chill for the rest of the night. Set your voicemail up so that they know you'll be ready about twelve o'clock tomorrow.

The O G Pimp From West Palm Beach, Part I

The next day, Papa told Will, "Pay for the rooms for another day."

After getting a few more dates set up for some anal Baby Girl started the show. The first date fucked her in the ass the entire time and came all over her. She showered and waited for the next date afterwards. When he came he said, "I want two girls." So Papa told Princess to go with Baby Girl to handle some business.

A few hours went by and the girls came back to the room with Papa's money.

"What y'all do to him?" Papa asked.

"We just went in and tag-teamed him," Princess said.

"She sat on his dick while I sat on his face. We went to work on him. Then he told me to eat Princess out so he could fuck me in the ass doggy-style. Then Princess bent me over and ate my pussy until I came. Then he fucked her from the back, and when he was about to cum I opened my mouth to catch every drop. Then Princess deep-throated him while I sucked his balls. He stood over us while putting his dick back and forth in our mouths. He started jacking off and we got into the sixty-nine until the both of us came. Then he licked our cum up until we were bone dry."

And like a thief in the night, Papa and the crew stole away before sunrise. "We're going home. Baby girl is coming with us."

"Where is home?" Baby Girl asked.

"Singer Island."

Back at Singer Island Papa got Baby Girl her own apartment and clientele as well. Papa got a call from a date needing some girls but wanted to take them on a boat. "Hell no," Papa responded. "But y'all can get a room."

"Alright," The anxious date agreed.

Papa set it up. It took no time to get rolling once the crew arrived at Singer Island. Then Papa got a call from one of his girls.

"My date is flipping out. He beat me up and put me out of the room."

"Will, go to the Best Western to see what's going on."

After Will got there, he talked to the John. "This bitch smoking up all my crack. And she ain't doing shit. No fucking, sucking, nothing. So I put that bitch out."

Sweet P. got all her shit and went back to her room at the Sands Motel. Papa called her and told her, "I'll be there in a few." Then hung up.

Papa and Will met at the Sands Hotel and went to Sweet P.'s room. Off the muscle Papa told Will, "Check this bitch."

The O G Pimp From West Palm Beach, Part I

After Will did his duty, Papa asked her, "Are you hungry?"

"Yeah," She answered. So he went to get her something to eat.

He ordered some drinks from downstairs, then told her, "Stay in your room and get some rest."

Papa took all the dope, money and left her with a little weed to smoke. He sent someone else over to chill with Joe at the Best Western. That was just good business practices. Something a real pimp knows a thing or three about.

About the Author

Write to author Kevin Guyton "Big Papa" at:

KEVIN GUYTON #75264-004
Federal Medical Center
POBox 14500
Lexington, KY 40512

To order additional copies of this book or copies of Part II, please send check or money order to:

Midnight Express Books
POBox 69
Berryville AR 72616

QTY ORDERED

_____	THE O G PIMP Book I	$12.95	$_____
_____	THE O G PIMP Part II	$12.95	$_____
		Subtotal	$_____
How many books are you ordering	_____ x $3.99 =		$_____
		TOTAL ENCLOSED	$_____

Ship to:
NAME _____

ADDRESS _____

Made in the USA
Columbia, SC
31 January 2023